W9-BSD-463

DISNEP

Featuring
Buzz Lightyear
from Disney·PIXAR's
Toy Story 2!

What Makes a Hero

By Irene Trimble

A Random House PICTUREBACK® Book
Random House 🏠 New York

Copyright © 2003 Disney Enterprises, Inc. *Toy Story* copyright © Disney Enterprises, Inc. Tarzan® copyright © 2003 Edgar Rice Burroughs, Inc.,
and Disney Enterprises, Inc. Tarzan® owned by Edgar Rice Burroughs, Inc., and used by permission. *101 Dalmatians* copyright © 2003
Disney Enterprises, Inc. Based on the characters from the book *The Hundred and One Dalmatians* by Dodie Smith, published by The Viking Press.
All rights reserved under International and Pan-American Copyright Conventions. Published in the United States by Random House Children's Books,
a division of Random House, Inc., New York, and simultaneously in Canada by Random House of Canada Limited, Toronto, in conjunction with
Disney Enterprises, Inc. RANDOM HOUSE and colophon are registered trademarks of Random House, Inc.
Library of Congress Control Number: 2002110091   ISBN: 0-7364-2159-9
www.randomhouse.com/kids/disney
Printed in the United States of America   10 9 8 7 6 5 4 3 2 1

What makes a hero?

A hero always swings into action when
someone needs help.

A hero keeps trying even when the odds are against him. Heroes never give up!

A hero knows that no challenge is too big . . .

. . . or too small.

There are a lot of ways for a hero to
show his courage. Whether it's by
facing the jaws of a snapping hyena . . .

. . . or by tasting something new, a hero is always brave.

A true hero always stays cool—even
when he's in a hot situation!

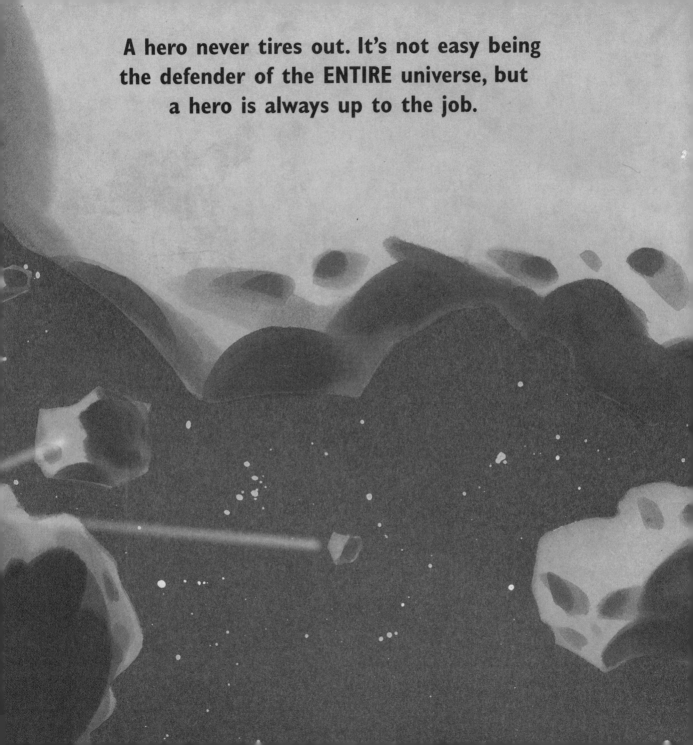

A hero never tires out. It's not easy being the defender of the ENTIRE universe, but a hero is always up to the job.

A hero never runs from danger—even
when time is running out.

Heroes come in all shapes and sizes.
Sometimes the biggest heroes come in
the smallest packages!

A hero is never afraid to take things over the edge . . .

. . . but sometimes even a hero needs a helping hand.

A hero sets a good example for everyone.
Every hero inspires you to be the best you can be.

And anyone can tell you—a hero is not measured by the size of his strength . . .

. . . but by the strength of his heart.